Intense Encounters

T. T. Morgan

MW01534031

Intense Encounters
T.T. Morgan
© Copyright 2008
Cover Artists: Eric Young Promotion Lotion
Interior design: Hanh Le - Broken Heart Studio

All rights reserved. No part of this book may be reproduced or transmitted in any form or by any means now known or to be invented, electronic or mechanical, including photocopying, recording, or by any information storage or retrieval system without written permission from the author or publisher, except for brief inclusion of quotations in articles or reviews. This is a work of fiction. The events and characters described herein are imaginary and are not intended to refer to specific places or living persons. The opinions expressed in this manuscript are solely the opinions of the author and do not represent the opinions or thoughts of the publisher.

Erotica/Short Stories
ISBN: 978 0 578 00120 3

Maine Stream Publishing Co.
http://www.mainestreampublishing.net

Maine Stream Publishing and the "MP" logo are trademarks belonging to Maine Stream Publishing Co.
Printed in the United States of America

Acknowledgments:

I would like to give thanks to the many people who helped me so much in making a dream a reality.

Joy – for being better than the best friend I could have ever wished for. Thanks for your unconditional love, your extraordinary kindness, your everlasting support, and your stunningly beautiful smile! You make my world a better place!!!

Jay – thanks for always knowing what are the right things to say and when to say them. You have helped me through things without knowing it many times! And thanks for giving this baby a name!!!

Dre – thanks for your support and unconditional friendship, and the special birthday gift which got it all started!

Jermaine Rivers – thank you, for believing in me, your help, your patience, your encouragement and your support.

Contents

page 1 ⸺⸺⸺⸺⸺⸺● A trip to Canada

page 5 ⸺⸺⸺⸺⸺⸺⸺● Quickie

page 9 ⸺⸺● Another travel tale - Amsterdam

page 19 ⸺⸺⸺⸺⸺● A secret meeting

page 29 ⸺⸺⸺⸺⸺⸺● Hit and Run

page 33 ⸺⸺⸺● A night at the Laundromat

- Saturday Night-

page 47 ⸺⸺⸺⸺⸺⸺● Damn Liar

Intense Encounters

T.T. Morgan

For the men in my life ...

A Trip to Canada

I get off the plane in Toronto and you are there to pick me up. You are tall, handsome and sexy ...and it feels so very good seeing you - I am excited, butterflies in my stomach and you give me this wonderful tight hug and a nice kiss. You smell so good and I want you, I want you so badly right now! The ride to the hotel seems to take forever, we talk, we laugh, we kiss, and we finally get there.

You have arranged for a beautiful room with a wonderful big bed and a huge tub in the bathroom. I unpack - you order room service and I take a shower ...I come out of the bathroom with a towel on - that's it, you are looking at me.....I walk towards you ....I can't wait to feel you - to kiss you and touch you all over your body.....to taste you and lick you all over.

You reach out to me as I drop my towel and you grab me by my small waist ...pull me towards you, you kiss my flat stomach and my tight breasts, play with your tongue with the piercings in my nipples - your lips feel so good. I had been waiting to feel your tongue for so long. You kiss me and before you can get to my sweet pussy with your tongue, I lean over and make you lay back onto the bed on which you have been sitting on. I pull up your shirt and start kissing your stomach, run my tongue around your navel up to your chest and play with your nipples. I suck on them lightly, I kiss your neck, your ear, and just as you want to turn your head to me to kiss me, and I make my way back down your stomach.

I start licking softly down your right side, pull down your pants and shorts, until I reach your groin area, I keep playing with my tongue until I reach your beautiful strong and perfectly shaped dick. You are so very hard. I lick your dick ...lightly up and down the shaft, getting it wet, very, very slippery. I circle the head with my tongue before I put it in my mouth. I start sucking on it ...just very lightly. My lips run up and down on it. I take it as deep as I can - you moan and that is such a turn on to me ...to feel that you are enjoying this. It gets me so wet; I could suck on you for hours.

All I want to do is make you feel good - I traveled all this way just to make you feel good, no – I want to make you feel great! I run my tongue up and down on your dick, I start licking your balls and put them in my mouth,.....playing with my tongue on them, ...little circles ......you pull me up, kiss me - I can feel your tongue, soft, wet; your lips feel so good on mine.

You push me on my back - look into my eyes ...you have that little smirk on your face,.....that little smile and that wink in your eye, as you start kissing my neck and work your way down on me past my breasts, my stomach, my navel. Until you reach the spot, you are trying to go to.

You kiss me - softly, lick me - gently, without being too eager to get to the one tiny spot you are trying to reach with your tongue

Finally ...with the tip of your tongue you reach between my pussy lips and touch my clit! It feels so good; I have waited to feel this for so long, so many months! I dreamt about it – often! The way you made me feel, back in Germany in that hotel room in Frankfurt when we first met, when you were there for the big championship game. I loved the way you made me feel then and I know you are about to make me feel the same way again.

You lick my clit, softly, with an even rhythm. Then you apply just a little more pressure, you lick it up and down, up and down, finally you start sucking on it and that is all it takes to make me cum so hard!!!

I just let it go - I don't want to control it – I squirt my sweet juices all over your face, your chest - you just made me explode! You keep going. I am so sensitive, but you keep going ...you are making me cum again, and again...

You keep at it with your wonderful soft tongue, licking and sucking on my clit and it doesn't take long and I cum right into your mouth again. I want you - NOW!!!!

I want to feel you inside of me, all of you - deep and you come up and look into my eyes as you slide your big, hard dick right into my dripping wet pussy effortlessly, it is hot in there, it is tight, and it has been waiting for you for so long. You look at me and you smile. You feel so good - hard, so excited. You go slowly, in and out, deep, all the way into it. I am so wet; you fill me up so completely.

You put my legs over your shoulders so you can reach all the way into my hot pussy - all the way to the bottom.

Now you start going faster and a little harder, then you stop, pull your dick out - turn me over and pull my ass up and towards you,.....looking right at my tattoo, ...looking at my nicely shaped big ass, holding on to my small waist, sliding your dick right back into my pussy.

I was just waiting for that. This way you can reach even deeper. You start going harder and faster, then you want to slow down again, you want to make it last, longer, just a little longer, but I beg you - yes, I beg you NOT to stop. I am so close! I want to cum on your dick! You keep going and going, you hit it harder and harder and faster and faster, and I let it go. I cum on your dick so hard! You feel it, how wet I got, how hot I got. You cannot hold it any longer and you cum right inside of me.

As you lie down on top of me and kiss me on the back of my neck and my ear, I moan and you whisper, "Welcome to Canada, Babe!"

I wake up; reach for my cell phone, which is plugged into the charger laying on the nightstand. The clock says 8:55 am. "Time to get up" I think to myself. I roll over one more time and look around in this room, which is not very familiar to me. I have never been in here before last night. I see the TV, a dresser with some books on it, a couple of nightstands.

The wineglasses and empty condom wrappers from last night are still present on one of the nightstands. I smile to myself as I let the events of last night pass through my head. He called me, he was upset, he needed a friend to talk to, and the good friend I am I hurried over there in the middle of the night with a good bottle of wine. When I got there, he was obviously pissed off.

We sat, we talked, he started to relax, he started smiling and laughing again. We drank some wine, actually, we drank the whole bottle of wine and he leaned over and looked at me and then he started kissing me. For a while now I had wondered what that would feel like, but I respected his situation and his ties. I sensed his attraction to me, but he was not available, so we did not act on this impulse.

Now, that the situation had changed I allowed myself to find out what his kisses feel like. They were soft, gentle, and passionate. One thing led to another, it got steamy and passionate, and after a few good climaxes, we fell asleep next to each other.

So here I am, looking around in his bedroom. He left early this morning for work and I have to get up in a few minutes.

Suddenly I hear footsteps in the hallway, a key that turns in the lock. Next thing I see, is him walking into the bedroom. He has a big smile on his face.

"Good morning" he says, "Did you sleep well?"

"I did" I reply as I roll over onto my stomach and the cover slides off me. I am completely naked. He looks at my round ass and my legs, just bare on the bed. "It just makes no sense." He says as he makes his way over to the bed. He puts both of his hands on my ass and just rubs it gently.

"Mm, mm, mm...don't go anywhere I'll be right back" he smiles as he leaves and I hear him going into the bathroom to take a shower. I pick up the cover and cuddle up with it, I am still tiered, and it was late last night. I feel myself starting to doze off again. When he returns a few minutes later, all he wears is a towel and many tiny water drops on his athletic body.

I only have a few seconds to look at him. Sexy, handsome, a stunning smile, well defined shoulders and arms, nice chest and a sexy six-pack. He comes back to the bed, climbs on top of me, and starts kissing my neck, my ears, and my cheeks... licking me gently and tickling me with his strong tongue. Before I even realize what is really going on he gets under the cover and buries his head between my legs.

Very gently, he starts to lick my pussy. He uses one hand to part my pussy lips just enough so he can gently stroke my clit with his soft tongue. He is doing it gently and softly and after last night, that is exactly the right approach. I shiver,

"Right there" I say, "Just like that". He follows my instructions and keeps licking me with gentle but firm strokes. Up and down, up and down. It doesn't take long and I feel myself getting closer and closer to climax. "Faster!" I moan, "Go faster!" His tongue starts flicking faster and faster over my clit. I use my hands to pull my pussy lips open so he can get to my entire clit. I feel it swelling under the wet, gentle, and fast strokes of his tongue. He stops!

"Don't stop!" I moan, but he just stops licking to start sucking on my clit gently and that's all I need to cum hard right into his mouth. I let a little scream out, "Damn, that felt great" I say, as I am looking right at him.

"That's what I want" he replies, "what better way to start the day, huh?"

He reaches for the box of condoms on the nightstand. He kisses me and then leans back so he can put the condom on his beautiful big and hard dick. I look at him, his body is wonderful. Just looking at him turns me on and makes me tingle even more in anticipation. I touch his chest and just slightly pinch his right nipple, "mm" he moans as he leans toward me.

I grab his dick and slide it into my pussy. "Mmm, so hot, so tight" he whispers and he starts to stroke my pussy with his big, hard, and strong dick.

He starts slowly and I can feel him deep inside me. He feels great. So big! His size is just perfectly filling me up. He keeps stroking and stroking, my legs are up against his chest. He grabs my ass with his right hand and pushes himself even deeper inside me. His strokes are getting faster and faster and I squeeze his dick with the muscles inside my pussy.

Faster and faster he goes, in and out, short deep strokes,... He starts to breath heavy,..."Give me that dick" I whisper. He looks at me, smiles and starts to fuck me really, really hard. It only takes a few more seconds and I can feel him explode inside of me...

"Good morning." I say with a smile on my face. "Yea" he replies, "a quickie is a great thing sometimes."

Another travel tale
~ Amsterdam ~

*S*o the trip to Amsterdam was not as nice as I had wished. The meetings were long, the topics dry and the discussions stressful. Only one more day and then I get to fly back home... In the little spare time I had, I wandered the streets of Amsterdam by myself. What a beautiful city. What a shame I had no one to share this beauty with. It could have been so much fun.

I wandered around and saw the sights, the shopping areas, the beautiful architecture, the Canals, even ventured into the red light district. How sexual, how bizarre and some of it so sensual, what a shame that I was alone. The meetings were over and it was my last night in Amsterdam. It was cold and windy, and it looked like it would start raining any minute. Two days before New Years, oh I was so ready to go home!

Before I return to my hotel for the last lonely night in Amsterdam, I decide to stop at the information & service desk at the central train station to check on the departure time for the train to the airport in the morning. It was just after 8 pm, still so many people in the streets and at the train station. I make my way to the service desk; the man is friendly and efficient, just the way I like it, and he actually smiled!

I turn around and make my way back to the main exit. As I stop to put on my gloves I see HIM coming across the street towards the door I just came out of.

He is tall, dark, young, and handsome. Black pants, black shirt and jacket, as he walks by me he looks right at me, his eyes warm and friendly and his smile breathtaking!!! WOW!!!

I smile back! It seems like I just stand there looking at him for an eternity, but in reality it cannot be more than a few seconds - he speaks. Just a simple "Hello"

"Hello!" I say, he stops and says, "How are you?" "Good, you?" I answer. He still smiles...wow, what a breathtaking, warm smile.

He says, "My name is Mike and you are?"

"Swept off my feet" I want to say, but I am just thinking i... instead I say "T... my friends call me T."

"Well T," he says, "where are you going?"... "Nowhere really" I reply.

We are standing there, looking at each other, smiling and while it feels exciting and tantalizing, the situation has something strangely familiar and comfortable. I have not felt something like that in a while... a good feeling, I don't feel the cold or the wind. "It's early and you have nowhere to go, have you had dinner, yet?" he asks.

I smile, thinking about the fact that I had planned on stopping at McDonalds on the way back to the hotel... hahaha life is amazing sometimes..."No" I say "Where are we going?"He looks at me and then he says

"How about a nice steak?"

"Let's go" I say, and with that we start walking next to each other towards Dam Square. I take his arm... nice! I feel a strong bicep, a tight body, and muscles... nice!

We start talking, he lives in Amsterdam, originally he is from Surinam in South America, his English is excellent, I tell him a little about me, why I am in Amsterdam, how the past three day were boring and lonely in such a beautiful city. He smiles. Out of the corner of my eye, I see him looking at me... checking me out.

"Damn, why could I have not met him three days ago" I catch myself thinking. I try to check him out, he looks very athletic, and I try not to be too obvious. We walk across Dam Square, into a small street, there on the left is a "Gauchos" we step in, it's Saturday night, the place is packed. The Maître d' informs us that we will have to wait about 15 minutes for a table.

We wait at the bar, we talk, we laugh, our table is ready in less than 5 minutes, and it seems like we are old friends catching up with each other's life. We sit, we talk... the waitress has to come back 3 times before we are ready to order, I look at him, he has broad shoulders, a small waist, very nice strong but gentle hands, full and soft looking lips, beautiful teeth which make his smile so gorgeous.

He looks at me; I can tell he wants me. I know he is imagining what I look like under my clothes. We are flirting with each other....he feeds me his salad. I know he wonders what my lips feel like... my tongue... as I lick off the salad dressing from the fork. I am having so much fun, He touches my hand, and it sends shivers through my body, what a great encounter. Half way through dinner I catch myself starting to imagine how his body would feel close to nine, I wonder if he is a good kisser.

He must be... he simply must be! His lips look so delicious! His conversation, his wit, his charm, all of it makes me just want him! After dinner, we are not ready to part ways. We decide to have some drinks and walk through some narrow alleys to an Irish pub. There we sit at a table, right in front of the fireplace and order a beer and a glass of wine, stare into each others eyes as we talk the night away... wow,... it feels like I have known him for a long time... I sit there, I listen to him, and all I can think about is how his lips would taste.

I want to kiss him so badly. I am having these visions about his lips and his tongue. Restless I move in my chair,... feeling how I get wet in my panties... just thinking about the things I want him to do to me... how I wish he would just lean over and kiss me... soft and gentle... wet and long and passionate.

Only when the lights come on do we realize how time flew by... 3 am and we have to go. We leave the pub and start walking back towards the central train station. My hotel is only a few minutes walking distance from there. He walks me all the way back to my hotel, on the steps we stand, looking at each other. He holds my hands; he leans forward and kisses me gently... FINALLY!

I feel a tingling in the pit of my stomach... it moves further down ... and I can feel the tingling in my pussy. I am getting so wet just feeling his tongue play with mine. His soft lips caressing mine, his hands around my waist, touching my butt, holding me close. I can feel him getting excited, his breathing starts getting heavier; I can feel his dick getting hard. He is pressing his body against mine.

It is still cold out here, but we do not feel it anymore. I am so excited,... I can feel my heart race,... I'm looking at him, so close to me,... I can smell his cologne,... he smells so good,... so sensuous. I feel his strong arms around me. I turn around, away from him and holding on to his hand I start to walk up the stairs to the hotel entrance. We enter the lobby and make our way to the elevators.

He follows me, not saying a word. He just smiles; it is a gentle, seductive smile... almost like a little shy smile. Finally, the elevator doors open, we get in .and I am wishing my room would be on the 99th floor, but that is just wishful thinking. The elevator stops on the third floor. Not even enough time for one good kiss!

He follows me without a word. I open the door to my hotel room, I can feel my heartbeat in my throat, I know that once the door closes behind him I will be able to make some of the visions I have had all night a reality - what an exciting thought! I hear the door snap into its lock; I unbutton my coat, take it off, and throw it over a chair, my gloves, and my scarf end up in the same chair.

He takes off his jacket. I am so eager to see what is under that black shirt. I want to see his muscular tight body. He steps towards me and pulls me close to him, his kiss is passionate and deep, his lips soft and gentle, his tongue is wet and warm, and I can feel how badly he wants to taste me. He starts to unbutton my shirt, looking into my eyes, and then he starts kissing my neck. I feel his tongue move down my neck, soft and gentle licks ... little kisses all the way to my collarbone. My breathing gets heavier, my heart races, and my entire body tingles.

My shirt just drops to the floor, with just one hand, he unbuttons his shirt in a hurry, and I can finally see his muscular chest, his broad shoulders, and his strong biceps. He holds me close as he kisses me passionately. I take a step back, I want to look at him, and I touch his chest, his abs, and his arms. His skin is so smooth, soft, yet his body so firm, his muscles so hard. My hands wander to his belt buckle, open it and then I unbutton his pants, unzip the zipper, and let his pants fall to the floor.

Gently I slide both of my hands into his boxer briefs from behind, across his ass cheeks, nice and firm and round. I let my hands glide down further and with my hands going down, so are his boxer briefs. I am getting down on my knees so he can step out of his shoes, the pants, and underwear. My face right in front of his beautiful fully erect dick! I am looking up at him and see him looking right into my eyes, he looks almost helpless, just standing there naked, he places his hands on my shoulders, and I take my eyes off his face and look at this beautiful dick right in front of me.

I touch it with my right hand. I hold it and start stroking it slightly, he lets out a little moan, I hold on to it just a little firmer. My mouth getting closer, my lips touching the head of his beautiful big dick! My tongue making little circles on the head of his dick, I am licking him gently, then my tongue makes its way down his shaft, easy, long, wet sloppy licks, down his shaft all the way then back up, from all sides, I am getting his dick wet, so very, very wet.

I look up at him. His head is slightly tilted back, his eyes are closed his mouth slightly open and he his breathing heavier. The whole time I am licking his dick I am stroking it gently with a firm grip of my hand. Slowly I am starting to suck on the head of his dick, he shivers, I hear another slight moan, then I finally take his dick into my mouth, slowly at first but then I take it as deep as I can and I can feel it all the way at the back of my throat.

He lets out a moan – louder this time. I stroke his dick with my mouth, suck on it, play with my tongue with it, I take it deep and feel his body tremble, I take it deep and deeper and just when he thought I couldn't take it any deeper I take it all the way down my throat. His knees buckle slightly, I can feel his hands grabbing my shoulders... I hear him say"... damn, girl, damn, damn! "

As I look up at him I see him looking right at me, he smiles, he pulls me up to him and kisses me, his tongue playing with mine, flicking it up and down as if he is trying to show me what he can do with it. I am getting excited just at the thought of him exploring my body with his tongue.

He unbuttons my jeans and I step out of my shoes. He pulls my jeans down and I sit down on the edge of the bed. He gets on his knees right on front of me as he pulls down my tiny and soaking wet panties.

Gently he pushes my legs apart. He starts kissing the inside of my thighs; I can feel his warm and soft tongue licking its way toward my pussy. He is teasing me, going slowly, making his way closer and closer finally touching my pussy lips. His one hand caressing my left booty cheek while his right hand is gently touching my outer pussy lips, he lets his tongue slide through his fingers and finds its way between my pussy lips; slowly he is moving it up and down making its way deeper into my pussy.

His hand expertly pulls my pussy lips apart and he starts licking my throbbing clit. Very gently, he touches it, I moan! He licks it again, just the right pressure, gently, soft not hard, he licks it up and down and up and down and it seems like he reacts to every little movement of my hips. I look at him, the way he pays so close attention to the way my body reacts impresses me.

I close my eyes and let my body go; I lie on my back and give in to the feeling of pleasure. I am so confident that this sexy black man has only my pleasure in mind. At this moment, I can feel him sliding two fingers effortlessly into my wet pussy, curving them up slightly finding my G-spot. Gently he massages it while his tongue keeps licking my clit.

His movements become a bit faster, still gentle but the flicks of his tongue are becoming much faster and faster and before I know it, I reach my first orgasm. I cum so hard and I have to grab a pillow to cover my mouth so that the hotel guests next door do not hear my lustful screams. When I open my eyes, I see him standing up, looking at me a warm and caring look in his eyes. He gets into the bed and pulls me close to him.

He kisses me, I can taste myself on his lips, I lick them, and he says, "You taste so sweet!" He leans over me and runs his hands across my breast, my stomach reaches down to my pussy, puts a finger deep into it, pulls it out and sticks into my mouth. I smile while licking off his finger and I say:" I do!"He kisses me and moves really close to me. I feel his skin, warm, soft, I can feel his dick throbbing, strong, and hard and I want to feel him inside me badly!

He looks deep into my eyes and I feel his dick sliding right into my wet pussy. "Oh God" I moan... he feels so good; he fills me up so completely. This man's body is hard, but his dick is even harder. His movements are perfect. I wrap my arms and legs around him in a lustful embrace that obviously turns him on. He pushes his dick deep into me; he moves in long and rhythmic strokes, I can feel him so deep.

His wide dick is rubbing me in spots I have not had touched in a long time. His strokes are getting faster and shorter... he is pumping into me with quick, deep thrusts and I am starting to feel pleasure I have not felt in a long time. "Don't stop, please don't stop", I beg him.

All of a sudden, his fast breathing stops, he is holding his breath. His muscular back tightens up. I am getting so excited, I know what is next... I can feel his dick jump inside of me. At that moment he slows down... he starts to breathe slow and controlled, smiles and says, "Oh, damn... you almost got me." He kisses me and I feel him pulling his throbbing dick out of my pussy.

He pulls away from me and with a little smirk on his face he says in a caring, but firm tone of voice: "Turn over!" I turn over on my stomach and without him asking I move my big, round and soft ass up into the air, towards him. My face buried in the pillow, my back arched, just waiting for him to get behind me... to grab my ass cheeks with his strong hands and to stick his big throbbing dick back into my wet dripping pussy. I do not have to wait long... I can feel him get onto his knees. I can almost feel him looking at my ass. I feel his hands grabbing my ass cheeks, spreading them wide, he is looking right at my wide spread open pussy. I can feel my juices running down the inside of my thighs. Just the thought of him sliding his big dick back into my juicy pussy any second now makes me tremble, I can hardly wait.

Then I feel it – with one deep, quick, and hard stroke, he rams his hard throbbing dick deep into my pussy. He goes as deep as he can, I moan, I did not expect him to enter me with so much force. He grabs my small waist with both of his hands and pulls my ass closer to him. He starts to fuck me... hard... powerful strokes... deep, oh so deep then I feel him putting one hand on the middle of my back... pushing me further down into the pillow while the other hand is pulling my ass higher into the air and closer to him.

He is stroking my pussy with long and deep and hard strokes...filling me up so completely, touching me in spots I haven't been touched in a while, he bends down over me,... kissing me behind my ear,... licking my neck, sending shivers down my spine,... he whispers: "Shit girl,... your pussy feels so damn good."

As he lifts up from my back, I can feel him grab my hair and pull it firmly back towards him. His stroke has slowed down and the change of the movement is giving me great pleasure... then again he surprises me as he starts to fuck me again hard, deep, pulling my hair and I love the force this man is using on me. Not many men dare to be dominant with me.

He finds the perfect balance between gentleness and dominance and as he fucks me so hard and so deep I feel my pussy tightening and twitching, I finally let myself go and cum on this beautiful hard dick. I cum so hard that I can feel myself squirting all over his dick, my cum is running down my legs and drenching his dick and balls,... now there is no stopping him anymore. He pulls his dick out of my soaked pussy, turns me over quickly by my shoulder, and pushes me down backwards into the pillow. He leans over me and I have this beautiful throbbing dick right in front of my face. He comes closer and I start sucking his dick. I can taste my cum, and it turns me on.

It is sweet and juicy and now he starts fucking my mouth. I feel his dick all the way down my throat, I feel the veins in his dick throbbing in my mouth,... I can taste the pre-cum and just as he cums he pulls his dick out of my mouth and cums all over my face, all into my mouth, onto my tongue. I lick the last drop off the head of his dick as it is coming out. He tastes so good. He moans, his eyes roll back and he almost collapses on top of me. As he recovers and lays down next to me, holding me in his strong arms, smiling at me... all I can think about is coming back to Amsterdam – soon, very soon,... not soon enough!!!!

A secret meeting

*H*e left **Luxembourg early that morning** on his way back to the States. We both knew that this was the last time we would see each other for a while. Over the past few months, we had become friends, cool friends. We laughed together, joked around together, and drank together and shared stories, interesting, fun and very intimate stories. We had fun. He is a nice guy, young, very young, tall, dark and very handsome with an athletic body, good head on his shoulders, a lil on the wild side, but still a good guy.

So here I am, parking my car at the Frankfurt airport, his lay-over is more than 6 hours. Enough time to meet up, have some breakfast, and hang out together one last time. I smile as I look in my rearview mirror, just checking my make-up before getting out of the car. I wear a short black skirt, sheer black thigh highs, black 3 inch pumps and a tight white t-shirt, neither panties nor bra.

"I need to remember to keep my knees together." I think to myself with a little chuckle, I grab my leather jacket and my purse before locking my car. With confident steps, I walk through the parking garage towards the elevators. Getting in I pull out my phone. As always, I am running a few minutes late.

"Where are you?" Reads the text message I am sending. By the time the elevator door opens, my phone vibrates in my hand. "Terminal 1 at Starbucks." reads the answer. I smile, my heart rate slightly increases... no one but me and him know about this meeting none of his friends, not my best friend....this is our little secret.

The past few months we flirted with each other so much – but we never acted on the sexual tension which had built up so tremendously over the many times we seen each other. So this secret meeting just adds to the excitement of our acquaintance. As I walk towards Starbucks I see him sitting there, his back turned to me, his long legs stretched out, he is sitting in one of the comfortable big chairs.

He heard the clicking of my heels and before I could reach him, he turns around and smiles at me. "Hello Sunshine, I thought I recognize that sound," he says as he gets up to give me a tight hug. He kisses me on both cheeks and then he looks at me close and he just leans over me so very slowly and his lips touch mine.

They are so soft and I feel a tingle in the pit of my stomach "Wow" I think to myself. After all this time imagining, I finally feel what they taste like. I open my eyes and I see that his eyes are closed, he ever so slowly pulls back, and I could swear that I felt his heart race. His eyes open – he looks at me and there was this wonderful smile of his.

"Wow", he says, "You have no idea how long I have wanted to do this"... his usual playfulness had disappeared and he sounds so serious and sincere. "Sit" he says..."how are you? What do you want to drink?"

"I'm good. Get me a Cappuccino, please" I reply. As I sit down his hand brushes up against my shoulder and neck as he walks towards the counter to order my cappuccino. Another little tingle, this time down my neck and back... Only a few minutes later he returns with my coffee.

"There you are. Enjoy!" he says as he puts it down in front of me and pulls his chair really close next to mine and sits down.

"Thanks, boo boo", I laugh, that is what I called him for the past few months, and we always had a good laugh about that.

As I start sipping my cappuccino, I can feel him looking at me. From my feet up to my hair... I catch him lingering with his eyes at the lace of the thigh highs, which was peaking out a little at the seam of my short skirt.

"You look gorgeous, as always!" he says.

"Thank you, sweetie" I reply. I can feel how he starts to get a little nervous, so unusual for him, I think to myself. He is the confident black male, who is not moved by anything, but there he sits and I can definitely feel how he is a little nervous. This is the first time we spent time one-on–one. No one else around; No friends, no loud music, no groupies... just him and me so we start to chit chat a little.

First about his trip going home, the past season, new friends made, the fun we had together over the past few months and how nice it is to encounter real people on our way through life. His hand slowly starts to reach over, inch by inch until it finally ends up on my thigh, his pinky finger plays with the lace of my stockings. There is that slight tingle in the pit of my stomach again.

"Let's go have breakfast," he says, giving my thigh a soft squeeze. "Let's go across the street to the Sheraton, they serve great breakfast and it's not so loud and not so many people around!" "Ok" I say as he gets up and reaches his hand out for me to grab as I get up. He picks up his small carry-on, I grab my purse, and we make our way to the exit.

It is cold out here so early in the morning; it is around 7:30 am and the weather here in Frankfurt is typical for a German April day, cold, rainy, windy, the usual.

"This I won't miss," he says as he puts his arm around me to make sure the wind does not get me too bad. We walk across the street and in a matter of 2 minutes reach the entrance of the hotel. We make our way towards the restaurant. The smell of fresh croissants and bacon puts a smile on our faces. The hostess seats us in the back of the restaurant, away from the buffet, in a quiet corner... just the right spot for us.

Together we get up and make our way to the buffet to get some food. Breakfast is my favorite meal of the day. I fill my plate with eggs and bacon, some hash browns, a croissant, some butter and strawberry preserves. In a small bowl, I put some fresh strawberries and cream. All along, I can feel him right behind me, looking at me, smiling and whenever I happen to look at him, he looks straight into my eyes

He just seems happy to have this opportunity for us to spend some time alone together. He is too cute. Many times have I imagined how it would be to spend a little time together, to know him a little better...closer. I am enjoying this, the attention he is giving me, the obvious desire in his eyes turn me on.

"We should have done this a while ago" I catch myself thinking...looking at him as we walks past me to make his way back to our table. I am right behind him. The loose clothes he is wearing hide his very athletic body well, but I know what is underneath the baggy jeans and the long Polo Shirt. I have danced with him before, we have shared many hugs, and I have had plenty of opportunity to feel what is under all of it.

I never felt his skin but I always thought that it would be smooth.

"What are you thinking about?" he asks, "What is that smile all about?" "Hmmm", I laugh. "I cannot tell you that right now, maybe a little later. Enjoy your food".

The table is small and we sit so close to each other that our elbows touch every now and then as we eat our breakfast. I can feel his legs touch mine under the table and there is that little tingle in the pit of my stomach again.

I can feel how I start getting moist between my legs; a warm sensation fills my body. We are truly enjoying each other's company and talk and laugh about things we experienced together over the past few months. Hanging out with friends in different clubs, bars, and a little drama here and some funny situations there. I am dipping a strawberry into the cream and then into a little bit of sugar.

"Want some?" I ask.

"Hell yea!" he replies, "not just the strawberry though!" He winks at me as I feed him the sweet strawberry and he starts licking my fingers, gently he takes my hand in his and starts kissing the inside of it. I can feel his soft tongue licking the palm of my hand as he runs little circles with the tip of his tongue.

"Hmm!" I moan, now the tingling wanders from the pit of my stomach further south and I feel my body getting warmer. I have chill bumps on my arms and I can feel my nipples under my tight T-Shirt getting hard. I lean towards him and he starts kissing me softly, so very gently. His lips are sweet from the sugar on the strawberry; I can feel his soft and wet tongue making his way between my parted lips.

"Wow" I catch myself thinking again, but then I can hear myself say it out loud: "we should have done this some time ago!"

"I agree." he says and gives me a little wink. "Don't go anywhere, I will be right back", he says as he gets up and disappears in direction hotel lobby. I sip on my freshly squeezed orange juice and when he comes back, he sits down.

"Any more sweets for me? Sweetie?" he asks.

"What would you like?" I reply as I look towards the buffet.

"What I want is not over there, it's sitting right here in front of me." He smiles and I see a sparkle in his eye.

"Oh really? Is that right? Well, a little late, don't you think? Our timing is messed up!" I reply.

"It's never too late, sweetie." And with those words, he gets up, reaches for my hand, and pulls me out of the chair. "Come with me" he says and I follow him without a word. We leave the restaurant and make our way through the big hotel lobby. Just as I want to turn towards the exit he leads me around the corner to the elevators

"This way!" he explains and shrugs his shoulders "I figure we would like to spend a little time away from everyone, so I just got us a room. I still have about 5 hours before my flight starts boarding. We can just chill, maybe take a nap. What do you think?"

I look right into his eyes and reply, "I think that this is a great idea!" The elevator door opens and he shoves me gently into it from behind. I can feel his big hands cup my bootie cheeks "So soft, damn girl". I hear him whisper.

He pushes the button for the seventh floor and corners me in the back of the elevator, his arms to the left and right of me he leans over me and gives me a deep soft and very wet kiss. I love the way his tongue feels, how soft and gentle it is and how he moves it around in my mouth, caresses my lips with it, plays with my tongue.

His right hand makes its way down my back and he squeezes my ass, then his hand reaches a little further under my skirt and he feels my soft skin, from behind he reaches for my pussy expecting to feel some panties, but all he feels is my wetness and my smooth skin. He slides one finger between my pussy lips and enters my body... I let out a little moan as he pushes his whole body against mine. I can feel how his dick is getting hard and he starts to breath a little heavier.

The elevator door opens and he pulls me down the hallway towards the room. I am so looking forward to what is already happening in my mind right now... "Take a nap" I think to myself..."yea right, whateva!!!" We reach the door and he opens it, I step into the room and he follows me. At the moment I hear the door shut I throw my jacket over a chair. I feel his hands around my waist as he turns me around; he starts to kiss on me again – passionately, as he leads me further into the room. I feel the bed in the back of my legs and as he leans over me, I sit down on it.

For the first time I see him take off his shirt. "What a great body!" I think, as I watch him... dark smooth looking skin, nice chest, small waist and a tight six-pack. My hands reach out for his chest – I want to touch his skin and it feels as smooth as it looks. Looking at the bulge in his pants, I cannot help myself but to think about what he will look like completely naked. He gets on his knees right in front of me and slides his hands on the outside of my thighs under my skirt.

He keeps pushing my skirt up until my pussy is exposed, he leans forward,... his soft lips and wet tongue start kissing the inside of my right thigh and he makes his way to the spot in the dead center between my legs. His tongue feels so soft, so warm, and so wet. Very gently he starts licking the outside of my pussy... I lean back, on my elbows, just far enough to relax, but not too far! So I can still watch him do what he is doing to me... I love to watch!

He looks up at me and smiles. "You like?" he winks and gets right back to what he was doing. This time his tongue explores a little deeper and with a gentle touch, he uses his right hand to part my pussy lips. Then I can feel the tip of his tongue on my clit and with soft up and down strokes, he starts licking it... I moan.

What a great feeling... my body starts to shiver slightly. I am-watching him, I see how he truly enjoys giving me pleasure, I can feel and see my clit getting bigger and I can feel it getting harder. He is doing his thing and he is doing it so right, my body responds to everything he does to it. Now he starts flicking his tongue up and down a little faster... and then just a little harder.

I can feel my first orgasm coming on, so quickly, and so hard! "I'm cumming" I moan and as I do, can't hold myself on my elbows any longer. I fall back and my legs start to tremble. I cum so hard and I can feel my juices run down my inner thigh. After a few seconds, I open my eyes and I see him standing there. He is licking his lips "damn gurl, you taste good!" Again, he smiles as he opens the belt on his pants, his jeans drop to the floor and within a second, he gets rid of the shorts and steps out of his shoes.

"Now that's a beautiful sight!" I say as I am looking at him standing right in front of me. He has a wonderful athletic body with a beautiful, perfectly shaped huge dick!
He is fully erect and I can see a little drop glistening at the tip of it. I sit up and reach right for it. It feels strong, hard, and so smooth. I lean forward and start licking his entire shaft up and down with my long wet tongue.

Then I start licking the head of his dick in small circles and when I hear him starting to breathe a little heavier, I put my lips around the entire head of his dick. "Hmmm... damn!" I can hear him moan "shyt, that feels good!" I take him in deep, as deep as I can. I can feel him all the way in the back of my throat. I suck on him; my lips tightly around his entire dick... I go up and down and up and down... his knees starting to shake just a little bit.

I use my hands and my mouth and I got his dick so wet that

the juices are running down his balls and my hand. I have a nice rhythm going and just when he least expects it I take him in deep - all the way down my throat. "Fuck!" he moans loudly as his knees buckle. "Stop... you have to stop! I can't take it... it feels too good and I am not ready to cum, yet. I want to be inside of you, feel your wetness on my dick!"

And with that he pulls back from me, pulls my T-shirt over my head and my little skirt down my legs. "Leave the pumps and the stockings on," he says", you look so sexy! I like that shyt, turn around!" he tells me and I obediently oblige him and turn over onto my stomach. He kneels behind me, putting his hands on my ass cheeks... then I can feel him spreading them apart and for a second he is just looking at the view.

Then I feel his hard dick effortlessly sliding right into my wet dripping pussy. This time he is not that gentle, he thrusts his dick deep into my pussy. "Damn!" I burry my face in a pillow and push my ass towards him. He fills me up completely, he feels so good, so hard, and he reaches so very, very deep. All this is much more than I ever imagined. He strokes me hard, in, out... deep, long strokes. I am touching my clit, rubbing on it, first gently, but as I can feel his dick getting even harder, I rub on my clit a little harder. I can feel myself cumming again and I know he can feel my pussy tightening up. His thrust are getting shorter, faster, harder, deeper,... I throw my ass back at him and within seconds I can feel myself cum on his dick, I almost scream.

I cum so hard that I feel my cum squirting on his dick, running down my legs and his. I can feel his dick explode inside of me. I hear him moan, loud and breathless!

I look back at him and this time I smile. "You like?" I ask. "Why did we wait so long for this? Damn... we could have been doing this for months!" he almost sounds angry, I laugh at him.

"Now you have something to think about all summer." I lay down on my stomach, he lays on top of me, starts to nibble on my ear, kissing my cheek, I tell him to place a wake up call before we take a nap. When the phone rings, we don't have time for a second round. We both take a quick shower and get dressed before we leave the room and make our way back across the street to the airport.

We walk to the security check together, joking, playing around, there we stop, and he looks at me and gives me a big hug, a passionate kiss and a warm look into my eyes.

"You better keep in touch, lil' mamma! Take care of yourself." He says.

"I will, sweetie." I answer and give him another quick kiss on the lips.

"Go, don't miss your flight, be safe and I may see you soon." As he walks away and goes through the security check I stand there and watch this tall handsome man.

"What a wonderful experience, what a nice way to start out such a cold, rainy day." I think to myself and smile. I see him as he gets done with the security check.

He turns around, smiles, and winks at me one more time. I turn around and start walking away. I can feel him looking at me, looking at my ass, I smile..."Yeah! You will have a lil' something to think about over the summer!"

Hit and Run

I am at the bar trying to get the bartenders attention. As I am standing there, looking around I see him standing right opposite of me on the other side of the bar. He is looking right at me, staring at me. I smile, he smiles, and then he winks at me. "Cute smile". I think to myself "handsome, young, and sexy!"

The bartender takes my order and I get my drink in a matter of a few seconds. When I hand her the money she says "Already taken care of" and points at the guy across the bar. I toast to him and say "Thank you!" so he can read my lips. He nods smiles and as I read his lips he says:" I wanna fuck you!"

I smile, wink, turn around, and walk away. "Not a bad idea". I think to myself. The night is still young. I make my round through the club and say hello to a few people I know. It is a busy night, many people there, everyone is having fun. After a while, I make my way to the bathroom. All I want to do is powder my nose and put on some lipstick.

Only one other girl is in the bathroom with me. As I lean towards the mirror, she leaves. Only a second later the door opens and I do not want to believe my eyes - HE just walked into the ladies' room. The guy from the bar! He smiles, grabs my hand, and without a word pulls me in the last stall in the ladies' room. He locks it quickly and then turns towards me..."hey!" I want to say, but he just pulls me towards him and starts kissing me passionately.

His lips feel soft, wet, his tongue is strong and gentle at the same time, and I feel his hands reaching under my shirt, squeezing my nipples, playing with my piercings. His right hand reaching under my skirt, looking for panties, but all he feels is bare skin and as his fingers explore, another piercing, he slides two fingers effortlessly deep inside me.

The excitement got me so dripping wet, he pulls out and touches my lips with his fingers, and I lick them... then he licks them.

"You taste good," he whispers, as he pulls my skirt up and pushes me up against the wall. He bends down and buries his head between my legs; he goes right for my clit and licks it hard and strong with his soft wet tongue. I moan and hearing people come into the bathroom adds to the excitement. He is licking me fast and faster while sticking two fingers into my pussy and one in my ass.

My knees are shaking – I am about to loose control. When he starts sucking on my clit, I feel my first orgasm! I cum so hard right into his mouth; I look down and I can see my cum dripping down his chin. He is still licking my clit and within a few more seconds I cum a second time. His lips and chin dripping wet from my pussy juices he kisses me. "I just wanna fuck you so bad!" he whispers and turns me around and pulls my ass towards him.

I hear his zipper and the sound of him opening and putting on a condom. "Smart guy!" is all I can think before I feel him ram his hard and huge dick into me. "Fuck!" I moan "Damn, that feels good" and I can hear him starting to breath heavy. He is pounding me and I throw my ass back at him. I have an answer for every single stroke. I feel him deep - he is so huge, filling me completely. He is fucking me with long hard strokes, in and out... hard and rhythmic strokes.

I can hear voices outside the bathroom stall door. I know they hear us, but I really don't care. This guy knows what he is doing! "Shyt, that pussy feels good – it's so tight! So fucking wet, so hot!" He is keeping is voice down but I can hear him. He speeds up, his strokes are becoming faster, shorter, and I can feel his dick start throbbing inside my pussy. "Go harder!" I tell him and he does and in just a few more really hard strokes he makes my pussy cum on his dick and only seconds later I can feel him explode inside of me. His knees are shaking this time. He grabs me around my waist while his dick is still inside of me and pulls me close to him. He kisses me on the back of my neck. "Damn gurl, that was nice!"

He pulls out and flushes the condom down the toilette. I pull my skirt down and try to clean up a little, he smiles at me, winks. I open the stall door and walk past two ladies who are waiting to use the bathroom. They look at me a little funny...but who cares. I check my make up and make my way back into the club.

At the bar I order a drink, I feel someone really close behind me, then a hand under my skirt, stroking my clit, very gently this time. I recognize the touch right away. He pulls his hand out from under my skirt and pays for my drink. " What is your name?" I ask him. "Jason" he replies. I smile and walk away, "Nice" I think. "I may just have to get his number later..."

A night at the Laundromat
-Saturday night-

I really could imagine doing something more fun to-night. But I have to do what I have to do. It was a really hot day – so unusual for Germany. I waited and waited for the temperature to drop. My damn washer had to break this weekend, right?! Damn, it is always something...

I packed up my laundry in a couple of big duffle bags and a basket and hauled them to my car. Good thing the Laundromat on base stayed open 24 hours.

It was a little after midnight when I came through the gate. "Good evening, ma'm" says the Airman on guard duty as he reaches for my ID card.

I cannot see his face, he is tall, very tall, and from the distance as I pulled up slowly all I saw was that he is a black guy; seemed to be athletic under that uniform. I was just hot; it was still around 80 degrees in the middle of the night. So very unusual for Germany. I love the heat, but the thought of spending the next couple of hours at the steamy Laundromat was not a pleasant one

"Enjoy the rest of your night" I hear his smooth voice say, as he hands back my ID card and bends down a little – just far enough for me to see his face, his stunning smile.

"Nice, really cute!" I think to myself. I reach for my ID card - he keeps holding on to it, just for a second, just long enough for me to look right into his eyes, he lets it go...was that a wink???? Did he just wink at me? Or is my mind just playing tricks on me in this heat? "Hmmm" I think to myself, too bad I didn't run into this guy somewhere else, some other time..."

"I'll try" I reply to him as I notice him glancing at my legs. All I am wearing are some cut off shorts, a cut off T-shirt and some Flip-Flops. It was just a quick glance, a tenth of a second, but I caught it! "Hmm" I think to myself "I wonder what is on your mind." I put the car in gear and pull off, looking at him in the rear view mirror. I see him standing there, watching me take the right turn towards the Laundromat, and then as I come around the .

corner I can no longer see him

I smile to myself; "T, you got a wicked mind" I catch myself wondering what he looks like underneath that uniform. "Get your mind out the gutter", I remind myself that I am here to do laundry and nothing else! After parking the car, I carry the two bags and the basket full of dirty laundry into the Laundromat. There is an older guy smiling at me as I enter the place .

"Good evening young lady" he says and smiles.

"Good evening sir" I reply as I pass him and look for the washers I want to use.

I drop my bags, put down the basket, and return to the car to get all the supplies I need and a plastic bag full of quarters. I see the little old man watching me out of the corner of my eyes. "Men will be men," I think to myself smiling. I guess it really does not matter what age.

I smile at him friendly as I pass him a second time going back to my laundry. He is the only other person there besides me. People have better things to do on a Saturday night than coming to the Laundromat. As I am sorting my clothes and putting them into the different washers the older guy is packing up the rest of his things and leaving.

"Good night young lady" he says and winks at me. "Good night" I reply and keep sorting my laundry. I stop for a minute to get my iPod out and the earphones so I can at least listen to some music while I am doing this boring chore.

From where I stand, I can look out of the windows and door of the Laundromat. No air conditioning in here, only a couple of fans standing on each side of the room. I see a car drive by; I think it is a military police car, no other traffic around here.

Nothing else is open on this base in the middle of the night except the gas station and the 24- hour Shoppette and they are located on the other side of the base.

So, no need for anyone to drive by the Laundromat. I am listening to my music. Jill Scott just started singing:"I was just thinking about you..." I love that song, how she reminisces about a former lover who was so, so good to her but so, so bad for her.

Makes me remember this one guy I once knew. Mmm, mmm, mmm, it has to be the heat! Just listening to the music and thinking about this ex-lover of mine got me all hot and bothered. I can feel myself get wet and slippery between my thighs.

Ok, ok, back to doing laundry, Jill Scott is singing:" You just run across my mind, you just run across my mind..." I hum along and thoughts of freaky, wonderful extraordinary satisfying sexual explorations cross my mind.

I smile... Jill Scott sings: "How amazing... how amazing, when you would spread my limbs across continents," I smile, kiss this and this and this and this and that .hey..." she sings,... I love that song. Not that the song is any special song for me and an Ex, and me, no - it is, it's more like a song that brings sensual memories back to life." but in reality, honestly, I was never good for you and you were never good for me... I just remember what we used to do" she ends the song. I can hear her smile as she is singing those words. Good for her! Having memories like that to put to music, giving me, and millions of people a song we can dream with.

The last load I start are delicates. I hate doing my sexy lingerie here in these public washers. But I do not have a choice, so my different colored lace panties and thongs go into a garment bag and I drop them into the washer. I put quarters into the slots of each washer and push them in, one after the other. As I turn around, I glance at the door. Did I just see someone at the door?... I take the music out of my ear. I cannot see anyone. All I hear is the music in my earpiece and the old fans blowing shhhhhhh... shhhhhhh. The little breeze they provide feels really good.

I walk over to the door, everything is quiet, calm, and I see no one around. Down the street I see a couple of cars passing, going towards the gas station.

My music back in my ear I hear Joss Stone sing: "I need a little lovin' at least two times a day" I smile. Wonderful wishful thinking; I try to remember the last time I had some mind boggling sex and loving. I cannot remember. At least not right away. Then then I think of my trip to the Philippines a few months ago.

"Damn" I think to myself "it's been that long? No wonder I get all hot, wet, and slippery" I make my way to the car; getting out the newspaper, I brought to occupy my time with some reading. Something startles me, I cannot hear anything as the music in my ear is loud, but I could swear I just saw a shadow around the corner of the building. I look into that direction but cannot see anything.

I dismiss it. "No worries" I think to myself. "I am on base; the Police Station is right down the street. Nothing could possibly happen" I calm myself. I take my paper and walk back into the Laundromat. I am listening to Ledisi:" In the morning, will you be there in the morning, to love me, love, me..." The music calms me, I sit down kick off my flip-flops, and put my legs up onto the bench, my shorts are short, so part of my booty cheeks peak out of them.

My legs and arms are glistening from breaking a little sweat. It is still hot and the fans are only distributing the hot air. I stretch out on the bench, wiggling my perfectly pedicure toes... I read community news. What is going on around our base? Looking into the program of the upcoming Jazz Festival.

Again – I thought I saw someone outside the building out of the corner of my eyes. This time I saw the shadow clearly. It looked like someone was walking passed the front door. I am reaching into the pocket of my shorts looking for my cell phone.

I cannot find it. I must have left it in the car. I take the earphones out of my ears and turn the music off. I leave the paper laying there, put on my flip-flops, and walk back to the front door.

I look around carefully, "Hello – anyone there?" I speak out, not too loud. I feel like in one of those horror movies where the people should just get out of the house, but instead they just go looking for the monster..." Hahaha, silly me! Nothing is going on.

I am just imagining things!" I say to myself. I unlock my car door and bend over to reach for my cell.

"Nice view!" a smooth, deep voice says behind me. I almost have a heart attack!

"Fuck", I bump my head at the doorframe of my car, as I tried to stand up.

"Who the hell are you?" I hear myself saying angrily as I turn around. Then I see him standing there, this time in some shorts, tennis shoes and a wife beater. "I was right, he is very athletic under that uniform," I think as I look up at the guy whom I recognize to be the guy on duty as I was coming through the gate a while earlier. Broad shoulders, nice arms and chest, and judging from the way the shirt fits him I suspect a killer six-pack under it.

He is just standing there, a bag in his hand, just standing there blatantly looking at my ass and my legs, just smiling. Beautiful charming smile. He is not even trying to hide his stare. "Oh, haven't I seen you before? You are the guy from the gate, right?" I am rubbing the back of my head... that hurt!

"Right" he replies, his smile changes to a look of concern "are you ok? I did not mean to scare you like that. Let me take a look at your head." And with those words, he drops his bag and steps closer to me. He is tall, at least 6'5", he leans over me to examine my head where my hand was rubbing it. He smells clean, freshly showered, I smell a hint of Aqua di Gio by Armani, a very seductive scent. He puts his hand carefully on the back on my head, feeling for a bump, but there is nothing. His hands are big, strong, yet gentle. He rubs the back of my head, gently as he stands close to me and then he smiles again.

"Are you going to be alright?" he asks.

"I will be fine" I reply. I step away from him and turn back to my car. I bend down and reach for my cell phone. Again, I can feel him just staring at my ass. When I turn around, he is still standing there... big smile on his face.

"What? Something wrong?" I look directly at him.

"Hell no! Nothing wrong at all" he answers... I walk back into the Laundromat. He picks up his bag and follows me inside. I make my way over to the washers and check on the ones with my clothes. All along, I can feel him staring at me. I smile, "men are such visual individuals", I think to myself. I love their simplicity, when it comes to lust and their sexuality. I find it arousing to know that men function often by their most basic instinct.

I bend over to reach into one of the washers, very aware that by doing so I am giving him a better view of my ass and my booty cheeks just peeking out from under my very short, cut off shorts. If he stood a little closer and if he looks really hard, he would see my wet pussy starting to throb under the thin fabric of my shorts. "Maybe he can already see my wetness" and the thought of it gives me an incredible feeling in the pit of my stomach.

I turn around and reach for my laundry basket. His strong arm is reaching for it at the same time. "Let me help you" he says, and there it is again, that smile, that bright sexy smile. He bites his bottom lip, his head slightly tilted to the right. He comes closer and reaches into the washer, brushing up against my arm and my shoulder. A shiver runs down my spine. His skin feels soft, and there it is again, that seductive scent of his cologne. "Who puts on cologne to come to the Laundromat?" I think to myself. But I do not mind at all. He is just too sexy, and I am watching his strong arms reach into the washer and get out my clean laundry.

"Which dryer do you want this in?" he asks.

"Right over there" I reply as I point to a dryer I had checked out earlier. He carries the basket over there and I take two quarters out of my plastic bag. After he puts my cloths into the dryer, he closes the door and turns around. He just stands there, again smiling. "Thank you" I say as I try to reach up to insert the quarters into the slot of the machine. He is not moving. It seems like he wants to be in my way.

"You are so very welcome, sexy lady" and he bites his bottom lip again slightly. So I just reach over him, my arm touch ing his shoulder, my breast slightly brushing up against his chest. Immediately I can feel my nipples get hard. I am not wearing a bra, so I know he can feel them on his skin. I put the money into the slots of the machine, turn the knob, and push the "on" button.

He is not moving. I step back and as I want to turn around to get back to my laundry in the other washers, he grabs me around my waist. Gently he pulls me really close to him. "You are one sexy lady. What is your name?" I start laughing. I am having lustful thoughts about this handsome man and I just realized that I do not even know his name. "My name is T, what's yours?" I ask him. "I am Mike. It is really nice meeting you T."

I pull away from him and make my way back to the other washers. Just a few seconds later Mike is right next to me again. This time he opens an empty washer and puts his clothes into the machine. After putting in detergent, he closes the lid, inserts the required quarters, and starts the washer. Then he turns around, again looking at me. It is something about the way he looks at me, the way he smiles; it just gives me a tingle in the pit of my stomach. We chit chat a few minutes about where we are from, that we are both single, where we hang out and the fact that we have never seen each other before.

He helps me with moving my laundry from the washers to the dryers. When I grab my delicates out of the washer and take them to the folding table, open the garment bag to take out my lingerie, he looks interested.

"Nice" he says, as I pull out a pair of pink lace boy shorts. "Always matching?" he inquires.

"Always!" I reply with a smile and a wink. I wrap my lingerie into a clean, dry towel and put them into the laundry basket.

"So what color are you wearing tonight?" he smiles with a smirk on his face and I swear I see him licking his lips.

"I'm not telling you! That's really a little personal, don't you think?"

"Honestly, you are right, it's personal, but I am just dying to know" he winks at me.

He steps towards me and grabs me with both hands around my waist, picks me up and puts me on the table. His face comes close to mine and he whispers in my ear "I really think you are not wearing any panties, and I would just absolutely love to know".

He pulls back a little and his soft lips brush up against my cheek, he still holds me firmly by my waist and stands right between my legs. His scent is turning me on and I can feel my pussy getting dripping wet. Right at that moment, he looks down at me, right between my legs. I swear, as wet as I am he should be able to see it, but when I look down at myself I can not notice anything.

"You would like to know, huh" I whisper back, turning my head just a little, just enough for my lips brush up against his. His grip around my waist gets a little firmer, and as he starts kissing me softly, he pulls me all the way to the edge of the table. I can feel his soft tongue explore the wetness of my mouth, I kiss him back, and the kiss becomes much more passionate. This man knows how to work his tongue; his lips are soft and gentle.

I suck lightly on his beautiful bottom lip and as he presses against me, I can feel his arms, his strong chest, and his big hard dick against my hot body. His hands are moving down from my waist to my ass and with an even firmer grip, he pulls me even closer up against him. His kisses are such a turn on. I can feel my hard nipples rub against his chest. I know he can feel how hard they are and the thought of it turns me on even more.

My hands are around his waist and I am letting them run down his back to his firm ass. He kisses me down the side of my neck, he looks at me, as if to check and make sure that I am responding positively to his actions. I smile, let out a little moan as the tip of his tongue touches a very sensitive spot on my neck. "I really want to know," he says as he looks up at me and I feel him sliding his right hand into the back of my shorts. "I knew it!" he says triumphantly, "I just knew it! There was no way a pair of panties would fit under these."

He takes half a step back and lets his hand slide from my back to my stomach. With anticipation, I look at him. I am so excited that all I want is for him to finally touch my pussy. Feel the wetness, feel how my pussy is already throbbing at the thought of his big hard dick, I felt just a little while ago. He looks at me, like he is looking for my approval, and as I look back at him I close my eyes, tilt my head back a little and loosen my grip on his ass so he has more room to do what he is about to do. That's the sign he was looking for. He slides his hand from my stomach down to my pussy and as his fingers slide between my pussy lips, I hear him say, "Damn, you are so wet!" He starts to rub my pussy softly, I have chill bumps in this heat, and he rubs three fingers against my pussylips. I start to shiver, and then he takes one finger and presses it lightly against my clit. He can feel it swelling under the pressure.

As he starts to rub my clit slowly up and down, I moan, "this feels so good, Mike. Don't stop. Rub it Baby, rub it!" I lean back a little and spread my legs a little more. HE leans over me and kisses my neck, making his way down to my right nipple. Through the fabric of my shirt, I can feel this teeth nibbling on my nipple. Not too hard, not too soft, just right.

And before I am fully aware of it, he has made his way down to my stomach licking around my navel, still rubbing my clit, still getting me wetter and wetter, and driving me crazy. I forget that we are in a public Laundromat.

The table I am on is against the wall around the corner from the door, so no one driving by or walking by can see us but if someone walks through the door, they will get the full view.

Right now – I do not care. This man is so skillful with his hands and his tongue that that is all I feel, all I can think about. Still rubbing my clit and now using his left hand to spread my pussy lips apart slightly so he can get better friction with the finger of his right hand. His mouth going down, pass my navel now and as he stops rubbing my clit for just a second I can feel him pull down my shorts to my ankles.

I open my eyes; I look around, no one but us! I look at him and with a calming voice he says " Don't worry about anything, babes, remember, I'm a cop!" and then he puts his lips back on my stomach and starts to lick his way down to my dripping wet pussy. He looks up for a second, looks around and I get scared for a moment. Then he smiles, grabs his laundry bag from the table, and throws it on the floor. "Better for my knees" he laughs as he kneels down on it with his face directly in front of my pussy.

"It's real pretty, babes, it looks really good" then he licks it once... twice..."and it tastes sweet!" and then he spreads my pussy lips again and exposes my clit. Gently he starts licking it, circling his tongue around it. Touching just the tip of it, gently, I am starting to sweat; tremors are running through my body. He licks it slowly, steadily in an even rhythm, and as he feels it swell even more he slides two fingers into my pussy. Deep with even pressure, finds my G-spot and starts to stroke my G-spot without ever letting go of the pressure he has on his hand. Now he starts to move his tongue faster, still steady movements up and down, but just a little faster. I moan because I have not felt pleasure like this in a long time! This guy really knows what to do with his tongue. I am thinking about his dick, I cannot wait to feel it inside my mouth. I want to taste it, feel it throbbing against my lips.

Suddenly he changes his rhythm, he could tell by the way my clit was jumping, that I was getting close to climax. He puts my clit in his mouth and while sucking on it lightly he still flicks his tongue on it up and down, Just a little harder this time and a little faster. "Oh, damn... don't stop, baby please, don't stop! I'm cumming, babes, I'm cumming" and it takes only a few more licks and I explode!

I cum so hard that I feel myself squirting and as I look up, I see my juices run down his chin and chest. He kisses the inside of my thighs, slowly pulling his fingers out of my pussy. "That was nice," he says as he stands up. "Don't go anywhere", he turns around and reaches into one of the dryers that have stopped. He pulls out a couple of clean towels and comes back to help me off the table and clean up both, me and the table. I pull up my shorts and find my flip-flops, which I had just dropped, earlier.

He wipes down his face and chest with the second towel and as he stands there, face in the towel I take a step towards him and push him against the wall. With my right foot, I push the laundry bag, which is still laying on the floor, towards him.

He looks at me, surprised, and then he smiles. His body relaxes as he is leaning his entire back against the wall.

I get on my knees in front of him and look up at him. "What a powerful position" I think to myself, as I slowly pull his shorts down. I have anticipated this moment for a while. And the waiting was well worth it. I am rewarded with a beautiful, fully erect, circumcised, thick, and long dick. As I reach for it with my right hand, I see the little drop of pre-cum on the head of his dick already. Like a little pearl, just sitting there.

I look at it, then I look up at him, and I can see the look of anticipation in his eyes.

He says nothing, but I see him biting his bottom lip. I turn my attention back to the beautiful dick in front of me. And with the tip of my tongue, I lick that little pearl right off. I hear him breath loud! Slowly I start stroking his shaft up and down with my right hand, while with my left hand gently holding and massaging his balls. The tip of my tongue is circling the head of his dick, gently, just for a few seconds.

Then I start licking the sides of his dick with my entire tongue. I am getting it wet, very wet. He starts to move against the rhythm of my hand, pushing his dick deeper into my hand, I open my mouth, lick my lips, and let the head of his dick disappear in my mouth. "Mmm, shyt!" I hear him moan, I slide my mouth deeper down his shaft. My lips are firmly around his dick, sucking my cheeks to create a little bit of a vacuum to make it a tighter experience. I take him deep, all the way to the back of my throat.

He keeps pushing his dick deeper and deeper into my mouth.

I go slow, while still stroking him with the right and massaging his balls with my left hand. His dick is wet; I feel my spit running down my hand, my forearm, and his balls.

"Do you like it this wet?" I ask him taking his dick out of my mouth for just a second and wiping my chin. He just nods, "get that shyt, girl" He is looking right at me. He watches me put his dick back into my mouth. I stroke his shaft, up, down, up down; my grip gets a little firmer. My movement becomes a little faster. I suck gently just on the head of his dick, his knees just buckled.

I run my hand up and down his shaft and I stroke his dick with my hand all the way over the head of his dick. I lick his head with the tip of my tongue as my wet hand glides across the head of his dick over and over again.

"You have to stop, babes, please, stop! I want to feel your pussy!" and he almost pushes me away from him, pulling me up and in just a split second he bends me over a washer, pulls my shorts to my knees and rams his hard, huge dick into my soaking wet pussy.

"Hell, yea" is all I can moan "give it to me, babes, gimme me that dick" and I stand on my toes so he can reach even deeper. I feel him spreading my ass cheeks apart so he can get his whole dick deep into my pussy. I imagine what he is seeing and as I arch my back even more to spread my ass and pussy for him, I am rewarded by feeling him drive even deeper into me, taking my breath away. His strong hands dig into my hips as he fucks me hard and deep.

Then he changes his rhythm from long, hard, and deep to fast and very short strokes deeply inside of me. His wide dick is rubbing me in spots that have not been touched by a dick in a very long time. "I'm cumming babes, yes, just like that, I'm cumming!" I bite my lip to keep my voice down. I do not want to scream, but it feels so good that I cannot help it. I let out a short scream as I cum on his dick.

I can feel his muscular body tightening up, his breathing goes from fast to nothing, and he is holding his breath. As I turn my head to look at him, he has this intense look of pleasure on his face. I know what is coming next and the thought excites me. Feeling his dick jump inside of me, feeling every muscle in his body straining for release is such a turn on to me. He lets go of my hips and holds on to my shoulders, pulling me against him hard and rough, and in two more strokes I can feel him release.

He makes no sound, at first and then all of a sudden I hear him let out this incredible moan "Mmmmm, oh, baby... this feels so good!" He puts his arms around me and pulls me up. We are just standing there for a few seconds; he kisses the back of my neck and holds me tight around my waist. It is quiet in the Laundromat, all the washers and dryers have stopped, the only sound we can hear are the two fans... shhhhhhh... shhhhhhh...

Damn Liar

I am just sitting there, behind the steering wheel of my car. I know I must have a stupid look on my face. I hear the car behind me honk his horn, "damn",... I hear myself say out loud, "no way. He wouldn't do that!"... and as I put my car in first gear and finally pull off as the light already changes back to yellow I am thinking about what just happened.

I was on my way home from work, as I pulled up to this red light, my mind occupied with many things, music loud and as I looked to the right, I saw HIM! The guy I had been seeing for a couple of weeks. Nice guy, had potential for something a bit more serious, maybe. Or, so I thought when I first met him. He knew all the right things to say and made me feel special - Until he told the first lie!

I do not remember exactly what the lie was, but I do remember that it was something completely stupid, nothing even worth telling a lie about. Completely unnecessary! From that moment on, I realized that I could not believe everything he said. Not sure why he does this, just lie for no reason. Just like in this situation.

There he was, in his green BMW, talking on the phone, not looking my way. I see him smiling, handsome as he is. The light must have turned green; I am just sitting there, staring after his car as he pulls off... "wow", I look for my phone, dial his number and I hear it ring.

"Hey sweetie, how are you?" flirtatious he answers his phone.

"Hey Babes" is my reply. "I'm good, how are you? How is your business trip going?"

"Boring sweetie, very boring, I miss you. I wish I could have dinner with you." He flirts. "Yea", I say", too it's bad that you have to be out of town so far today." I try to keep my voice calm and friendly..."You bastard" I am thinking to myself, last night you told me that you would be out of town for the next two days on business and just a second ago you passed me right here at this light.

I feel myself getting a little angry, with him, but more with myself. I should have just left him alone when I caught him lying to me the first time. Such useless, unimportant things, why lie? I just do not get it! I tell him that I am on my way home and because I am driving, I have to hang up and I ask him to call me later when he gets back to his hotel room.

I can still see the back of his car; he keeps going straight as I am turning left towards my house. " Well" I am thinking to myself "too bad, this one almost had some potential. Guess I will just have to let it go." My feelings are hurt a little, because I felt a little something for this one... but I will get over it, I'm sure. As I am pulling up in front of my house, I have come up with the perfect plan for revenge.

"This he will regret – I'm sure – for the rest of his life! I will make him remember me forever!" I catch myself thinking aloud. I start smiling, a thought formulates in my mind, and as I get into the elevator in my apartment building and push the button to the penthouse I have made up my mind. I kick off my shoes, put down my purse and after I hang up my jacket I pull my phone out of my pocket, I look at it and with a little smirk I decide to turn it off!

The next afternoon my phone rings and by the number on the display, I can see that it is he. "Hey sweetie," I hear his charming, sexy voice", how are you doing? What happened to you last night? I tried calling you. I missed you so much! I just wanted to hear your sexy voice before I had sweet dreams about you.

Did you think about me a little? Maybe miss me? I have a surprise for you. I will be back in town in a couple of hours. I am already on the road on my way home. I really want to see you. I miss you so much and I can't wait to hold you in my arms, kiss your lips, and feel your touch." He really knows what to say.

"Hey babes," I reply, trying not to sound upset, "I miss you, too. I cannot to see you later. Drive careful. Dinner will be ready and waiting for you when you get here. So hurry." I hang up and shake my head; how can someone be so full of it. Why is he lying every time he opens his mouth? He has absolutely no reason to lie! The next couple of hours I spend with preparing dinner and getting the apartment ready.

I light up scented candles everywhere, fresh satin sheets in the bedroom and soft towels over the heater in the bathroom. Then I take a shower and get myself ready for a night like no other night ever. I have a plan and it is a sexy, sensual, passionate, and freaky little plan of revenge. It will be the sweetest revenge ever, but nonetheless it will be revenge and no matter how sweet, in the end it will hurt.

30 minutes later the doorbell rings, "It's me, sweetie," I hear him through the intercom. I push the buzzer; check myself in the mirror quickly. "Sweet," I think to myself. I am wearing a short black dress, heels and of course matching panties and bra. My hair is freshly washed and smells good; it flows long and wavy across my shoulders and my back and the blonde is in sensual contrast to the black dress. My face looks flawless, just a hint of mascara, and some lipstick.

I hear the elevator in the hallway, I open the apartment door, and he looks at me as he exits the elevator. "Wow, sweetie, you look good! You are so damn sexy!" with theses word he grabs me around my waist as he walks into the apartment, and pulls me close to him. He holds me tight and kisses me passionately. I can feel that he is excited, his dick is hard, and he presses himself tightly against me. I smile, pull myself away from him, grab his hand, and lead the way into the dining room.

Everything is ready, the salad is already on the table, the candles are lit, and the soft music is playing. I can see his eyes light up as he gets close to the dinner table. "Wow, babes, you really went way out to do all this. Looks like you slaved in the kitchen" he looks flattered "all this just for me? You must have really missed me." He says as he sits down.

I kiss him at the back of his neck, running my tongue just

lightly and softly behind his ear. "Anything for you, dear" I reply as I walk into the kitchen to get the white wine out of the refrigerator. I pour some in his glass, then in mine, and then I put the bottle into the little wine cooler. As I sit down across form him I smile at him, I can tell he is amazed. "Enjoy your meal, sweetie" I say just before I put the fork with a piece of tomato in my moth.

The dressing drips down the fork and I lick it off. I see him looking at me. I can tell his mind is wondering. We have been seeing each other a couple of weeks, we have passionately made out before, but we have never had sex. I know he has wondered, wondered how I feel, how I taste, what I look like when I get close to climax. All of this he will find out tonight!

While eating our dinner he flirts with me, he is so charming and sweet, so sexy! I cannot help but think about how wonderful it could be with this guy, if he would have not turned out to be such a pathological liar. He is sitting there, telling me about his business trip, how he missed me, how boring the city was and how bad the long drive was. All these lies, and I still do not understand why, and I do not care! All I care about is the fact that he lies, and he knows how I feel about liars. He is taking a chance by doing this. I have warned him before; I have explained it to him several times. However, I guess it is not important to him how I feel about that.

I look at him, listen to him, I smile, and while he finishes his last glass of wine I get up to go to the bathroom to start running the bath water. I hear him come into the bathroom. As I turn around, I see him standing there in the doorway.

"You are so damn sexy" he says and takes a step towards me. "You are really spoiling me."

"Sure," I reply, "you deserve it, right? You worked hard and then the long drive, you deserve to relax and be spoiled a little! I love treating my man the right way. Just imagine this treatment is something you can look forward to many more times to come." With these words, I turn around and turn the water off. The bathwater is full of bubbles and smells sensuous.

I turn to him get closer and start to unbutton his shirt, pull it off his shoulders, then I open his belt, unbutton his pants and pull the zipper down. The pants just drop. I get on my knees in front of him and help him step out of his shoe, pull off his socks and then, still on my knees, I pull down his boxer briefs. He is so excited, his dick his fully erect and I am looking right at it, his dick right in front of my face.

I look up, I smile, and he is looking down at me. It almost seems like he feels a little uncomfortable, standing in front of me, fully naked, fully erect with his big and beautiful dick. I touch it with my right hand, gently, yet firm. I rub it just a little. He lets out a little moan. Again, I look up at him, he has his head tilted back a little, his eyes closed.

I open my mouth, and very softly, I run my tongue across the head of his dick. "Hmm", I hear him moan; I kiss the head of his dick and give it one more gentle lick with my long tongue before I get up. He smiles, "you are wonderful, you make me feel great. I really think that this thing between you and I will be something very special." He gets into the bathtub.

I stand in front of the tub and start pulling my little black dress down over my shoulders. I let it drop to the floor and I stand there in my black bra, my tiny little black panties, and my black high heels. He is watching me, his eyes full of anticipation. I open my bra and let it drop to the floor; he is watching my every move.

I pull my panties down and stand there for a second in nothing but my high heels. "Come on, stop teasing me, get in here," he says. "On my way, sweetie" and I step out of my heels and step into the warm, bubbly water. I sit down across from him and smile at him "Hey, how are you feeling?" I ask him as I softly start rubbing his legs. He reaches out for me and starts caressing my legs in return.

The water feels warm and the bubbles are soothing. A sensual scent of lavender and roses fills the air. With his hands he rubs my calves, up and down, then across my knees, working his way to my thighs; Slowly moving from the outside to the inside of my strong and curvy legs. He runs his fingertips from my knees down the inside of my thighs all the way down to my pussy, just gently touching my outer puss lips.

He lets his fingertips run up and down on my pussy a couple of times. Then he leans back and just smiles at me. "You are so beautiful." He leans his head back and closes his eyes. I look at him. He is so handsome; he has a beautiful smile, athletic, sexy body. I find myself wondering how things between him and me could be if he could just tell the truth.

I shake my head, just slightly, "no need to wonder" I catch myself almost whispering to myself. I am not here to try to change this man. All I want is to make him remember me for the rest of his life. I lean forward and with my right hand, I touch his chest while keeping my balance by holding on to the bathtub with my left hand. My back is arched and my ass is sticking out of the water. I am on my knees, close to his face. He opens his eyes, again just smiling, not saying anything.

He leans his head forward just slightly and kisses me. He is such a good kisser. I catch myself wondering if he is just as good of a lover. I kiss him back; start licking the side of his neck with the tip of my tongue. He closes his eyes again and leans his head back. In little circles, I make my way down to his chest with my tongue. My tongue finds his right nipple and I just start sucking on in slightly.

I nibble on it and as I feel it getting a little harder I flick my tongue on it up and down, up and down, I feel it getting harder and harder. He moans, just a little, I smile. My right hand finds its way down his chest all the way down his abs until I reach his dick. He is completely erect and hard. The head of his dick reaches out of the water. He is big and fat just like I like it.

I grab him gently and start running my hand on his shaft up and down. Gently, very gently, I stroke his dick for a few seconds. My tongue reaches for his left nipple, I lick it and suck on it, and then I make my way down. I look at his dick right in front of my face and with the same circular motion, I start licking the head of his dick. Again, I hear him moan just a little. I cannot help but smile a little. His hands reach out to caress my shoulders.

He pulls my hair together behind my head with his left hand
He pulls my hair together behind my head with his left hand and with his right hand, he pushes my head down just a little. My face touches the water; I take a breath, open my mouth, and take his dick in all the way. I feel his dick go all the way down my throat. My face completely submerged in the water. I come back up for air and repeat the move one more time. When I open my eyes to look at him I see him staring at me. "How do you do that?" he looks surprised, almost shocked, but pleased, very pleased.

"That felt so good. I never experienced that before.
You are incredible, girl!" I move closer to his face, kiss his neck. He reaches for my ass with both of his hands. He squeezes my ass tightly. "Come on" he says, let us move to the bedroom. "Ok, babes, let's go". I stand up and he just looks at me. The water is running down my naked body, little droplets of water dripping from my nipples into the bathwater. I step out of the tub and reach for the warm towels hanging over the heater. "Stand up, let me dry you off".

He gets up and steps out of the bathtub. Then he stands really close to me. I can feel his hard dick almost throbbing between my thighs. He moves back and forth a little and his dick slides between my thighs and close to my pussy. I put the towel around his shoulders and rub his back with both of my hands; I dry off his chest and his stomach, and make my way carefully down to his legs and feet.

Kneeling in front of him, again I have his big beautiful hard dick right in front of my face. I kiss the head of it, just one time. I stand up and grab a second towel for myself. "Let me help you" he says and takes the towel from me. He turns me around and rubs the towel firmly, yet gently across my back and my ass. He bends down to get my legs and turns me back around so he can work his way up in the front.

He rubs the towel against the front of my legs, not missing a spot. He looks up at me, drops the towel, and grabs each one of my ass cheeks with one of his hands.

His face is right in front of my pussy. He puts his lips against my pussy and starts to lick it slowly. With the tip of his tongue, he parts my outer pussy lips and strokes my clit softly. It feels good; his tongue is wet, strong, yet so gentle. He licks around my clit just enough to make it swell a little. I can feel it get harder and I can feel myself getting wet, really wet. He moves his hands from my ass to the front. While still gently stroking my clit with his tongue he slides two fingers of his left hand into my hot juicy pussy and with his right hand, he pulls my pussy lips apart, to fully expose my clit. Now he starts to suck on my clit. I moan, it feels great and I know already that I will have much fun for the rest of the night.

I reach for his head and pull him up to my face. I kiss his lips and taste myself on him. He pulls his fingers out of my pussy and reaches for my lips. "Tasty, sweet" I say after I suck on them and lick my pussy juices off them. He has a look of amazement on his face. "You are something special. Come on, let's go next door" He grabs my hand and leads the way into the bedroom.

The light is dimmed, a few candles have been burning for the past couple of hours, and a sensuous scent is lingering in the air. I sit down on the edge of the bed and just look up at him standing there. "So handsome, so sexy, so naked." I think to myself, "Why can't his character match his looks? It is such a shame."Some things I do not have to understand.

He comes closer, leaning over me, he gets into the bed. As he reaches for me, I gently take his hand, "let me spoil you a little more" I say and I push him back into the soft comforter. He lays back, willingly, by now he knows that whatever I have planned for him will be lustful and pleasurable. I reach for the massage oil on the nightstand.

"Turn over sweetie, lay on your stomach, so I can get your

back."

I smile, and after he turns over, I get on top of him. I place my round ass on his lower back, my pussy still wet, I know my juices will flow onto his skin and that thought is a great turn on to me. The massage oil smells good, very arousing, I pour some in my hands and start to rub down his shoulders.

I feel his muscles and concentrate on the spots where I feel his muscles are tight. I get his neck, his shoulders, working my way across each arm. As I move my hands further down his back, I move my ass further down to his legs. I can see the wet spot my pussy left on his lower back. I know my pussy tastes good, so I bend down, and I put my tongue right on that spot.

I start kissing his lower back, licking off my own pussy juice with the tip of my tongue. "I taste good," I whisper, as I make my way down to his ass with my mouth. "Yes you do!" he answers in a soft voice "you are just a naughty girl. I love it!" I keep rubbing and massaging his muscles, my hands have a firm grip on his ass cheeks, and while I am still kissing and licking on him, I spread his ass cheeks just a little.

Just enough, to make a way for my tongue to touch a spot where no one else has ever touched him before. I hear him moan. I can feel him tense up a little, not sure of what I am about to do to him. "Relax, babes, I won't hurt you, I promise." I smile. I love to make a man feel things he has never felt before; make him experience things he only dreams about. Slowly I let my tongue wander deeper and deeper between his ass cheeks, until I feel the soft skin of his anus. My tongue just touches it lightly, just barely, with the tip of it.

He jumps a little, his body spasms, "damn girl, what are you doing to me? This feels incredible!" he relaxes, and I can feel him just letting go of all the tension in his body. His ass cheeks loosen up and I pull them apart just a little further. I start licking him in this sacred spot, pushing my strong, long tongue into him. He moans; I try to go deeper. He moans louder, almost like a soft scream. And as I bury my face deeper and deeper between his ass cheeks, I can feel him starting to tremble. I move my attention a little further down and lick his scrotum and the underside of his balls just lightly.

Then I sit up and continue to massage and rub his legs. First, his hamstrings then move my hands gently to the back of his knees, down to his calves. I massage both of his feet, "turn over, babes," I ask him. He willingly turns on his back. He looks at me. I can see the look of pleasure in his eyes. His arms are reaching for me. While on my knees, I bent down to him.

He hugs me, tightly, "you are an amazing woman. You do things to me and for me, no one else has ever done. You make me feel like I have never felt before... I love you!" he whispers and I look into his eyes. How I wish I could believe him!

I smile and pull away from his arms. I see him looking at me in expectation. He is waiting for me to return the declaration of love. I just smile and take the massage oil and pour some more into my hands.

"Relax babes. I am only half way done." And with those words, I start rubbing his chest. I massage his arms and come back to his chest, playing with his nipples and feeling the smooth oil on his soft skin. Again, he moans. I work my way down to his stomach and carefully massage his abs. His dick is hard and stands erect, pre-cum dripping from it onto his stomach. I lean forward, licking it off his skin. He shivers, and I concentrate with my hands on his legs, working my way down first his left and then his right leg.

"Now, to the good part" I think to myself. The thought of playing with his dick gets me excited. It gets me wet and I can instantly feel my pussy getting hot and slippery. I am dripping down my own thighs. With the rest of his body finished, I can now concentrate on my favorite part. I love a pretty dick! There is nothing more beautiful.

I lean forward and without using my hands I take his dick in my mouth and take it in as far as I can. I choke a little, but feeling his dick in the back of my throat just turns me on. His eyes open, he looks at me, "Baby, what are you doing? It feels so great!"

I run my mouth up and down on his dick, all the way from the head to the base. Up and down, with my right hand I start to play with myself. I want to feel his dick inside my pussy, but I am not ready to stop licking and sucking on it, yet.

My pussy is wet; I run my middle finger across my clit. I rub on it while I suck on this big dick in my mouth. I can feel my juices down my fingers, into my hand. I sit up for a second, pull my pussy lips apart with my left hand and rub on my clit harder with my right middle finger.

He looks at my face first, and then he looks at my pussy to see what I am doing. I love being watched. I am on my knees and I spread my legs a little wider so he can see a little better. I take two of my fingers and push them deep into my hole. I start moving them in and out, first slow, and gentle, then a little faster and harder. I like feeling the pressure, and I can feel myself shaking from lust.

"Cum for me, baby, come on, make yourself cum for me." I hear him whisper. His eyes are open wide. He watches me intensely, not wanting to miss a thing. I pull my fingers out, and start rubbing my clit again, harder this time, faster, much faster. I can feel the heat come up in the pit of my stomach.

"I'm cumming, babes, I'm cumming!" and after a couple more hard rubs against my swollen clit I cum so hard that I let out a scream. I keep rubbing, a little softer a little slower, just for a second and then I pick up the pace again and rub my clit hard, fast, very fast and once again within just seconds I cum again. This time all I can do is hold my breath! I let go of myself and look at him. He looks excited.

I climb on top of him, but instead of facing him, I turn my back to him. I take his dick with my right hand and slide it into my hot, swollen pussy. "Damn, it's so hot, so fucking wet, girl." He moans as I let myself down on it slowly. I take it in, all the way in, deep, as deep as it can go. I raise myself on his shaft, thinking about the visual he is getting behind, and I straighten my back and widen my base with my feet causing my ass to form that perfect apple look.

I slowly fuck him like that, my hands gripping and balancing myself on his thighs.

He is gripping my waist and slowly pumps his incredibly hard dick into me. The pleasure is immense, "Fuck me baby, I want you to fuck me please." I moan. His reaction is instant as he pivots his hips and dives so deep into me it causes me to scream out with pleasure while I grip his thighs and matches his thrusts.

He is getting faster and faster and I can feel his dick starting to throb inside me. As I cum again, I squeeze my pussy tight and that is all it takes. I can feel him explode inside me. His dick is jumping as he climaxes. I hear a muffled scream and as I turn around, I can see him bury his face in a pillow.

"Are you ok, Babes?" I wink at him, as I slowly lift myself off his dick. "I'm good. I better than good, I am great!" This was fantastic, Baby. This night I will never forget! I love you!" Again, I can see the look of expectation in his eyes. Again, I smile, and say nothing. That was exactly what I wanted to hear! I lay down next to him.

He grabs me, holds me tight, and starts to kiss me on my lips and my neck, looking at me. So I look at him and take it all in. How I wish I could believe him. He had so much potential, up to that first lie! As I lay there, I know this was the last time this man will pleasure me. I pull away from him, sit up; I smile...You have to go!" I say in a friendly, but very firm voice. "Huh?" he replied. He has this look of astonishment on his face. "I thought I was spending the night." He said in a pitiful tone. By now he could see how serious I was by the expression that was written on my face. His expression looked even more puzzled.

"No babes, you really have to go....!" I said as I stood up from the bed.

"Why?" he asked, and with some sadness in my voice, all I could reply is:

"I got what I wanted from you... besides I just can't stand a liar!"

Author Bio

T. T. Morgan was born in a small town in Germany. At a very young age, her family moved to Munich, where she spent her childhood and teenage years. After finishing school, she moved to the United States, living in Texas and Los Angeles. In 1990, she returned to Germany. For many years, she worked self-employed as a freelance writer for professional trade publications and as an Educator in the Beauty Industry. Before publishing her first book "Intense Encounters" she blogged her sensual stories on MySpace and continues to have thousands of faithful readers. She currently resides in Germany.

Printed in the United States
213315BV00004B/7/P